RAPUNZEL

AND OTHER FAIR MAIDENS IN VERY TALL TOWERS

Amelia Carruthers

ORIGINS OF FAIRY TALES
FROM AROUND THE WORLD

POOK PRESS

CONTENTS

An Introduction to the Fairy Tale 1

The History of *Rapunzel* 5

THE LEGEND OF SAINT BARBARA

(A Turkish / Lebanese Tale) 9

RÚDÁBEH

(A Persian Tale) 19

PETROSINELLA

(An Italian Tale) 29

RAPUNZEL

(A German Tale) 39

THE MAID AND THE NEGRESS

(A Portuguese Tale) 51

PRUNELLA

(A British Tale) 59

JUAN AND CLOTILDE

(A Philippine Tale) 73

The Golden Age of Illustration 83

An Introduction to the Fairy Tale

Fairy Tales are told in almost every society, all over the globe. They have the ability to inspire generations of young and old alike, yet fail to fit neatly into any one mode of storytelling. Today, most people know these narratives through literary works or even film versions, but this is a far cry from the genre's early development. Most of the stories began, and are still propagated through oral traditions, which are still very much alive in certain cultures. Especially in rural, poorer regions, the telling of tales – from village to village, or from elder to younger, preserves culture and custom, whilst still enabling the teller to vary, embellish or adapt the tale as they see fit.

To provide a brief attempt at definition, a fairy tale is a type of short story that typically features 'fantasy' characters, such as dwarves, elves, fairies, giants, gnomes, goblins, mermaids, trolls or witches, and usually magic or enchantments to boot! Fairy tales may be distinguished from other folk narratives such as legends (which generally involve belief in the veracity of the events described) and explicitly moral tales, including fables or those of a religious nature. In cultures where demons and witches are perceived as real, fairy tales may merge into legends, where the narrative is perceived both by teller and hearers as being grounded in historical truth. However unlike legends and epics, they usually do not contain more than superficial references to religion and actual places, people, and events; they take place 'once upon a time' rather than in reality.

The history of the fairy tale is particularly difficult to trace, as most often, it is only the literary forms that are available to the scholar. Still, written evidence indicates that fairy tales have existed for thousands of years, although not perhaps recognized as a genre. Many of today's fairy narratives have evolved from centuries-old stories that have appeared, with variations, in multiple cultures around the world. Two theories of origins have attempted to explain the common elements in fairy tales across continents. One is that a single point of origin generated any given tale, which then spread over the centuries. The other is that such fairy tales stem from common human experience and therefore can appear separately in many different origins. Debates still rage over which interpretation is correct, but as ever, it is likely that a combination of both aspects are involved in the advancements of these folkloric chronicles.

Some folklorists prefer to use the German term *Märchen* or 'wonder tale' to refer to the genre over *fairy tale,* a practice given weight by the definition of Thompson in his 1977 edition of *The Folktale.* He described it as 'a tale of some length involving a succession of motifs or episodes. It moves in an unreal world without definite locality or definite creatures and is filled with the marvellous. In this never-never land, humble heroes kill adversaries, succeed to kingdoms and marry princesses.' The genre was first marked out by writers of the Renaissance, such as Giovanni Francesco Straparola and Giambattista Basile, and stabilized through the works of later collectors such as Charles Perrault and the Brothers Grimm. The oral tradition of the fairy tale came long before the written page however.

Tales were told or enacted dramatically, rather than written down, and handed from generation to generation. Because of this, many fairy tales appear in written literature throughout different cultures, as in *The Golden Ass,* which includes *Cupid and Psyche* (Roman, 100–200 CE), or the *Panchatantra* (India, 3rd century CE). However it is still unknown to what extent these reflect the actual folk tales even of their own time. The 'fairy tale' as a genre became popular among the French nobility of the seventeenth century, and among the tales told were the *Contes* of Charles Perrault (1697), who fixed the forms of 'Sleeping Beauty' and 'Cinderella.' Perrault largely laid the foundations for this new literary variety, with some of the best of his works including 'Puss in Boots', 'Little Red Riding Hood' and 'Bluebeard'.

The first collectors to attempt to preserve not only the plot and characters of the tale, but also the style in which they were told were the Brothers Grimm, who assembled German fairy tales. The Brothers Grimm rejected several tales for their anthology, though told by Germans, because the tales derived from Perrault and they concluded that the stories were thereby *French* and not *German* tales. An oral version of 'Bluebeard' was thus rejected, and the tale of 'Little Briar Rose', clearly related to Perrault's 'The Sleeping Beauty' was included only because Jacob Grimm convinced his brother that the figure of *Brynhildr*, from much earlier Norse mythology, proved that the sleeping princess was authentically German. The Grimm Brothers remain some of the best-known story-tellers of folk tales though, popularising 'Hansel and Gretel', 'Rapunzel', 'Rumplestiltskin' and 'Snow White.'

The work of the Brothers Grimm influenced other collectors, both inspiring them to collect tales and leading them to similarly believe, in a spirit of romantic nationalism, that the fairy tales of a country were particularly representative of it (unfortunately generally ignoring any cross-cultural references). Among those influenced were the Norwegian Peter Christen Asbjørnsen (*Norske Folkeeventyr*, 1842-3), the Russian Alexander Afanasyev (*Narodnye Russkie Skazki*, 1855-63) and the Englishman, Joseph Jacobs (*English Fairy Tales*, 1890). Simultaneously to such developments, writers such as Hans Christian Andersen and George MacDonald continued the tradition of penning original literary fairy tales. Andersen's work sometimes drew on old folktales, but more often deployed fairytale motifs and plots in new stories; for instance in 'The Little Mermaid', 'The Ugly Duckling' and 'The Emperor's New Clothes.'

Fairy tales are still written in the present day, attesting to their enormous popularity and cultural longevity. Aside from their long and diverse literary history, these stories have also been stunningly illustrated by some of the world's best artists – as the reader will be able to see in the following pages. The Golden Age of Illustration (a period customarily defined as lasting from the latter quarter of the nineteenth century until just after the First World War) produced some of the finest examples of this craft, and the masters of the trade are all collected in this volume, alongside the original, inspiring tales. These images form their own story, evolving in conjunction with the literary development of the tales. Consequently, the illustrations are presented in their own narrative sequence, for the reader to appreciate *in and of themselves*. An introduction to the 'Golden Age' can also be found at the end of this book.

The History of

Rapunzel

Unlike many fairy tales, the classic 'Rapunzel' narrative actually has a reasonably short provenance. As the story of a beautiful young woman with long flowing hair, who – after a period of trials and tribulations finally reunites with her true love, it first appeared in print with Giambattista Basile's *Pentamerone* (1634 - 1636). This story, with the title of *Petrosinella* (meaning 'Little Parsley'), largely set the tone for all who followed, including the Brothers Grimm, Charlotte Rose de Caumont de la Force, and Andrew Lang. Despite this seeming creation *ex nihilo* though, there are some identifiable precedents which bear a striking similarity to Basile's tale.

The first of these is the legend of Saint Barbara, a third century holy lady who is thought to have lived in Nicomedia (present-day Turkey), or in Heliopolis of Phoenicia (present-day Lebanon). Her story was written down by Jacobus de Voragine, the Archbishop of Genoa (1230 - 1298) and published in the *Legenda Aurea* (1275). According to the legend, Barbara, the beautiful and intelligent daughter of a wealthy Pagan, was locked in a tower by her father – who intended to protect her from the world outside. During her time in captivity, she converted to the Christian religion and subsequently was tried before a court and eventually executed by her own father. Unlike later 'Rapunzel' narratives, Saint Barbara rejected proposals of marriage put to her by her father, instead focusing her devotions on the Holy Trinity of the Father, the Son and the Holy Spirit.

The second early precedent is the tale of Rúdábeh and Zál, from the ancient Persian epic, *The Shahmaneh* ('The Book of Kings'). This story, unlike the Legend of Saint Barbara is the first tale to mention the young maiden's long hair. Written around 1000 CE (and consisting of some 60,000 verses), the romance of Rúdábeh and Zál is recounted in the section devoted to 'The Age of Heroes'. Just as later versions of the heroine's name are highly significant, the word Rúdábeh comes from *Rood,* meaning 'child' and *Ab* meaning 'shining'; the shining child. Unlike Barbara, she is not kept in a tower against her will, but decamps there in order to meet with her true love, Zál. To allow him to climb up onto her balcony, Rúdábeh casts down her luxuriant hair, which Zál quickly ascends. All subsequent versions of the narrative (apart from the Philippine tale of Juan and Clotilde) mention the young woman's flowing tresses.

When considering these two tales in combination, it is easier to see how Giambattista Basile's *Petrosinella* came about. It contains the characteristic tropes of many later accounts, including the pregnant mother who craves some parsley from the ogress's garden. In the Brothers Grimm's story, this aspect is transformed into 'rapunzel' (a type of lettuce) taken from a sorceress, and in Andrew Lang's 'Prunella', it is plums, taken from a witches' orchard. From a scientific interpretation the 'evil' character can be portrayed as a witch or medicine woman, who had mastered the use of remedial plants capable of saving the mother from the complications of pregnancy. Such complications were of course, an incredibly common event in seventeenth century Europe. This seemingly uneven bargain (with the unfortunate woman's first born offered in return for the item of food) is a common trope in fairy tales; replicated in *Jack and the Beanstalk,* when Jack trades a cow for beans and in *Beauty and the Beast,* when Belle comes to the Beast in return for a rose. Folkloric beliefs often regarded it as quite dangerous to deny a pregnant woman any food she craved, and consequently family members would have gone to great lengths to secure such cravings. Such desires on the woman's part indicated a lack (especially prevalent in the lower, farming classes) of much needed vitamins – highlighting the tale's humble beginnings.

Basile's *Petrosinella* was subsequently adapted by the French aristocrat and writer, Charlotte Rose de Caumont de la Force (1654 - 1724), and published as *Persinette* (again, translating as parsley) in 1698. This version was incredibly similar to the original Italian, excepting that the ogress is this time a fairy, and the pair of lovers find their escape much more difficult. This French variant was then translated into German in the late 1700s, by Friedrich Schulz – a tale which then went on to inspire the famous Brothers Grimm. The Grimm's version has been chosen for this collection, due to its folkloric importance, and also for its similarity to the French tale of *Persinette*. Published in their 1812 *Kinder und Hausmärchen* ('Children's and Household tales'), its title, 'Rapunzel' is the name by which the narrative is presently known world-wide. Like De La Force, they also added in a more 'adult' detail, in Rapunzel becoming pregnant with the Prince's child (twins in the Grimm's case). Basile's story also described the prince and the maiden's encounters in quite bawdy language, but did not directly suggest pregnancy before marriage.

It was mature particulars such as this which drew criticism from the Scottish folklorist, Andrew Lang. Lang consequently referred back to Basile's original, but took the story in a different direction again, publishing 'Prunella' in *The Grey Fairy Book* (1900). In this version, Prunella is set a series of impossible tasks by the witch – but is aided in her endeavours by the witch's son, who only asks for a kiss in return. The good and chaste Prunella refuses each time, but eventually realises her true affections for the young man, after he kills his own mother (in order to save Prunella). Whilst still a rather gruesome ending, the murder of a wicked witch was considered more fitting for young audiences, than depictions of a young woman disobeying the orders of her elders, by giving herself willingly to the 'prince'. Like the strong-willed Saint Barbara, the 'Rapunzel' character is anything but a meek and obedient princess.

As a testament to this story's ability to inspire and entertain generations of readers, *Rapunzel* continues to influence popular culture internationally, lending plot elements, allusions and tropes to a wide variety of artistic mediums. Its classic line, of 'Rapunzel, Rapunzel, let down your hair!' has become an idiom of popular culture. The tale has been translated into almost every language across the globe, and very excitingly, is continuing to evolve in the present day. We hope the reader enjoys this collection of some of its best re-tellings.

THE LEGEND OF SAINT BARBARA

(A Turkish / Lebanese Tale)

The following legend was compiled by Jacobus de Voragine, an Italian chronicler and Archbishop of Genoa (1230 - 1298). It was published in *Legenda Aurea* ('The Golden Legend or Lives of the Saints') in 1275, first translated into English by William Caxton in 1483. The book was one of the most popular religious works of the Middle Ages.

Saint Barbara is thought to have lived in third century Nicomedia (present-day Turkey), or in Heliopolis of Phoenicia (present-day Lebanon). According to legend, her wealthy Pagan father kept her in a carefully guarded tower in order to preserve her from the outside world. Having secretly become a Christian during her captivity, Barbara rejects the offers of marriage put to her. The young woman is subsequently brought before a court and tortured for her faith, before being finally beheaded by her own father. These elements of the story are replicated in later narratives of 'Rapunzel', notably the girl locked in a tower, who only gains her freedom and salvation when she disobeys the orders of those around her, and the eventual punishment of the wicked jailer (in this case the father – analogous to the evil witch character).

$$\Longrightarrow$$

HERE BEGINNETH THE LIFE OF ST. BARBARA

In the time that Maximian reigned there was a rich man, a paynim, which adored and worshipped the idols, which man was named Dioscorus. This Dioscorus had a young daughter which was named Barbara, for whom he did do make a high and strong tower in which he did do keep and close this Barbara, to the end that no man should see her because of her great beauty. Then came many princes unto the said Dioscorus for to treat with him for the marriage of his daughter, which went anon unto her and said: My daughter, certain princes be come to me which require me for to have thee in marriage, wherefore tell to me thine entent and what will ye have to do.

THE TOWER WITH THREE WINDOWS

Then St. Barbara returned all angry towards her father and said: My father, I pray you that ye will not constrain me to marry, for thereto I have no will he thought. After this he departed from her and went into the town where there was one making a cistern or a piscine, for he had many workmen to perform this work, and also he had tofore ordained how he should pay unto each of them their salary, and after this he departed thence and went into a far country where he long sojourned.

Then St. Barbara, the ancille [handmaid] of our Lord Jesu Christ, descended from the tower for to come see the work of her father, and anon she perceived that there were but two windows only, that one against the south, and that other against the north, whereof she was much abashed and amarvelled, and demanded of the workmen why they had not made no more windows, and they answered that her father had so commanded and ordained.

Then St. Barbara said to them: Make me here another window.

They answered: Dame, we fear and dread to anger your father, which commanded us to make no more ne we dare not therefore make no more.

The blessed maid said: Do and make that I command you, and I shall content my father, and shall excuse you against him.

[...]

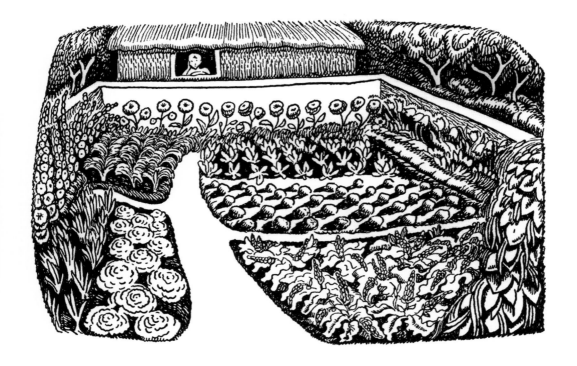

Often the woman would stand and look at this garden.
Tales From Grimm, 1936.
Illustrated by Wanda Gag

When he went over the wall he was terrified to see the witch before him.
Hansel and Grethel and Other Tales, 1920.
Illustrated by Arthur Rackham

On a time this blessed maid went upon the tower, and there she beheld the idols to which her father sacrificed and worshipped, and suddenly she received the Holy Ghost and became marvellously subtle and clear in the love of Jesu Christ, for she was environed with the grace of God Almighty, of sovereign glory and pure chastity. This holy maid Barbara, adorned with faith, surmounted the devil, for when she beheld the idols she scratched them in their visages in despising them all, and saying: All they be made like unto you which have made you to err, and all them that have affiance in you.

And then she went into the tower and worshipped our Lord. And when the work was full performed, her father returned from his voyage, and when he saw there three windows, he demanded of the workmen: Wherefore have ye made three windows?

And they answered: Your daughter hath commanded so.

Then he made his daughter to come afore him, and demanded her why she had do make three windows, and she answered to him, and said: I have done them to be made because three windows lighten all the world and all creatures, but two make darkness.

Then her father took her and went down into the piscine, demanding her how three windows give more light than two. And St. Barbara answered: These three fenestres or windows betoken clearly the Father, the Son, and the Holy Ghost, the which be three persons and one very God, on whom we ought to believe and worship.

Then he being replenished with furor, incontinent drew his sword to have slain her, but the holy virgin made her prayer and then marvellously she was taken in a stone and borne into a mountain on which two shepherds kept their sheep, the which saw her fly. And then her father, which pursued after her, went unto the shepherds and demanded after her. [...] And then her father took her by the hair and drew her down from the mountain and shut her fast in prison, and made her to be kept there by his servants unto the time that he had sent to the judge for to deliver her to the torments. And when the judge was advertised of the faith and belief of the maid he did her to be brought tofore him. Her father went with her, accompanied with his servants threatening her with his sword, and delivered her unto the judge, and conjured him, by the puissance of his gods that, he should torment her with horrible torments.

ST. BARBARA BEFORE THE PAGAN JUDGE

Then sat the judge in judgment, and when he saw the great beauty of St. Barbara, he said to her: Now choose whether ye will spare yourself and offer to the gods, or else die by cruel torments.

St. Barbara answered to him: I offer myself to my God, Jesu Christ, the which hath created heaven and earth and all other things, and fie on your devils, which have mouths and cannot speak, they have eyes, and cannot see, they have ears, and hear not, they have noses, and smell not, they have hands, and may not feel, and they have feet, and may not go, they that make them, be they made semblable to them, and all they that have fiance and belief in them.

Then became the judge all wood and angry, and commanded to unclothe her and beat her with sinews of bulls, and frot her flesh with salt, and when she had long endured this, that her body was all bloody, the judge did do close her in a prison unto the time that he had deliberated of what torments he might make her die.

And then at midnight descended a great light and clearness into the prison in which our Lord showed him to her, saying: Barbara, have confidence. and be firm and steadfast. for in heaven and in the earth thou shalt have great joy for thy passion, therefore, doubt not the judge, for I shall be with thee, and I shall deliver thee from all thy pains that any shall make thee suffer.

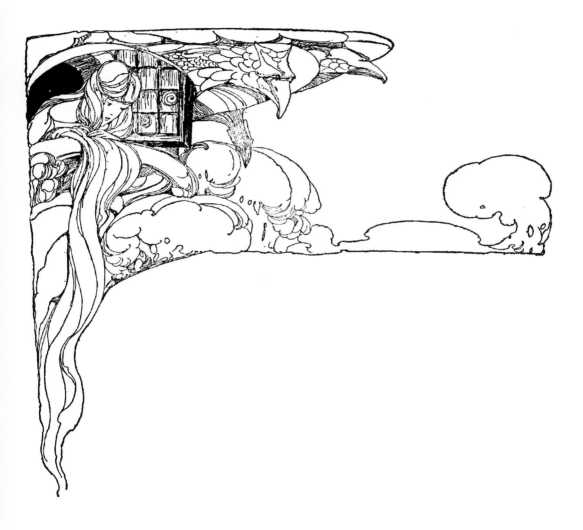

Rapunzel.

The Fairy Tales of Grimm, 1936.

Illustrated by Anne Anderson

[...]

And when she had long endured these pains, the judge commanded that she should be led with beating through the streets, and the holy virgin the third time beheld the heaven, and said: Lord God, that coverest heaven with clouds, I pray thee to cover my body, to the end that it be not seen of the evil people.

And when she had made her prayer, our Lord came over her, and sent to her an angel which clad her with a white vestment, and the knights led her unto a town called Dallasion, and there the judge commanded to slay her with the sword. And then her father all araged took her out of the hands of the judge and led her up on a mountain, and St. Barbara rejoiced her in hasting to receive the salary of her victory.

HER HOLY DEATH

And then when she was drawn thither she made her orison, saying: Lord Jesu Christ, which hast formed heaven and earth, I beseech thee to grant me thy grace and hear my prayer, that all they that have memory of thy name and my passion, I pray thee that thou wilt not remember their sins, for thou knowest our fragility.

Then came there a voice down from heaven saying unto her: Come, my spouse Barbara, and rest in the chamber of God my Father, which is in heaven, and I grant to thee that thou hast required of me.

And when this was said, she came to her father and received the end of her martyrdom with St. Julian. But when her father descended from the mountain, a fire from heaven descended on him, and consumed him in such wise that there could not be found only ashes of all his body.

Rapunzel sings from the tower.

Painting by Frank Cadogan Cowper, 1908.

RÚDÁBEH

(A Persian Tale)

Rúdábeh is a Persian mythological figure that appears in Ferdowsi's epic *Shahameh* – the 'Book of Kings'. Ferdowsi (940 - 1020 CE) was a highly revered poet, and his enormous poetic opus has become the national epic of the Persian speaking world. Consisting of some 60,000 verses, *The Shahnameh* recounts the mythical and to some extent the historical past of the Persian empire from the creation of the world up until the Islamic conquest of Iran in the seventh century.

The romance of Zál and Rúdábeh is described in the section of *The Shahnameh* devoted to 'The Age of Heroes.' Just as later 'Rapunzel' characters are described as dazzlingly beautiful maidens, the word Rúdábeh comes from *Rood,* meaning 'child' and *Ab* meaning 'shining'; the shining child. In this early version of the narrative, Rúdábeh is not held in a tower against her will, but decamps to her favourite palace in order to prepare for her first meeting with Zál. On his approach, she casts her luxuriant hair down from the balcony, which Zál quickly ascends – only after he has 'ardently kissed the musky tresses.'

→

The chief of Kábul was descended from the family of Zohák. He was named Mihráb, and to secure the safety of his state, paid annual tribute to Sám. Mihráb, on the arrival of Zál, went out of the city to see him, and was hospitably entertained by the young hero, who soon discovered that he had a daughter of wonderful attractions.

Rapunzel! Rapunzel! Let down your hair.
Tales From Grimm, 1936.
Illustrated by Wanda Gag

Her name Rúdábeh; screened from public view,
Her countenance is brilliant as the sun;
From head to foot her lovely form is fair
As polished ivory. Like the spring, her cheek
Presents a radiant bloom,--in stature tall,
And o'er her silvery brightness, richly flow
Dark musky ringlets clustering to her feet.
She blushes like the rich pomegranate flower;
Her eyes are soft and sweet as the narcissus,
Her lashes from the raven's jetty plume
Have stolen their blackness, and her brows are bent
Like archer's bow. Ask ye to see the moon?
Look at her face. Seek ye for musky fragrance?
She is all sweetness. Her long fingers seem
Pencils of silver, and so beautiful
Her presence, that she breathes of Heaven and love.

Such was the description of Rúdábeh, which inspired the heart of Zál with the most violent affection, and imagination added to her charms.

Mihráb again waited on Zál, who received him graciously, and asked him in what manner he could promote his wishes. Mihráb said that he only desired him to become his guest at a banquet he intended to invite him to; but Zál thought proper to refuse, because he well knew, if he accepted an invitation of the kind from a relation of Zohák, that his father Sám and the King of Persia would be offended. Mihráb returned to Kábul disappointed, and having gone into his harem, his wife, Síndokht, inquired after the stranger from Zábul, the white-headed son of Sám. She wished to know what he was like, in form and feature, and what account he gave of his sojourn with the Símúrgh. Mihráb described him in the warmest terms of admiration--he was valiant, he said, accomplished and handsome, with no other defect than that of white hair. And so boundless was his praise, that Rúdábeh, who was present, drank every word with avidity, and felt her own heart warmed into admiration and love. Full of emotion, she afterwards said privately to her attendants:

"To you alone the secret of my heart
I now unfold; to you alone confess
The deep sensations of my captive soul.
I love, I love; all day and night of him
I think alone--I see him in my dreams--
You only know my secret--aid me now,
And soothe the sorrows of my bursting heart."

[...]

But one difficulty remained--how were they to meet? How was she to see with her own eyes the man whom her fancy had depicted in such glowing colors? Her attendants, sufficiently expert at intrigue, soon contrived the means of gratifying her wishes. There was a beautiful rural retreat in a sequestered situation, the apartments of which were adorned with pictures of great men, and ornamented in the most splendid manner. To this favourite place Rúdábeh retired, and most magnificently dressed, awaiting the coming of Zál, whom her attendants had previously invited to repair thither as soon as the sun had gone down. The shadows of evening were falling as he approached, and the enamoured princess thus addressed him from her balcony:--

"May happiness attend thee ever, thou,
Whose lucid features make this gloomy night
Clear as the day; whose perfume scents the breeze;
Thou who, regardless of fatigue, hast come
On foot too, thus to see me--"

Rapunzel! Rapunzel! Let down your hair.
Fairy Tales From Grimm, 1894.
Illustrated by Gordon Browne

Rapunzel! Rapunzel! Let down your hair.
Old, Old Fairy Tales, 1935.
Illustrated by Anne Anderson

Hearing a sweet voice, he looked up, and beheld a bright face in the balcony, and he said to the beautiful vision:--

"How often have I hoped that Heaven
Would, in some secret place display
Thy charms to me, and thou hast given
My heart the wish of many a day;
For now thy gentle voice I hear,
And now I see thee--speak again!
Speak freely in a willing ear,
And every wish thou hast obtain."

Not a word was lost upon Rúdábeh, and she soon accomplished her object. Her hair was so luxuriant, and of such a length, that casting it loose it flowed down from the balcony; and, after fastening the upper part to a ring, she requested Zál to take hold of the other end and mount up. He ardently kissed the musky tresses, and by them quickly ascended.

Then hand in hand within the chambers they
Gracefully passed.--Attractive was the scene,
The walls embellished by the painter's skill,
And every object exquisitely formed,
Sculpture, and architectural ornament,
Fit for a king. Zál with amazement gazed
Upon what art had done, but more he gazed
Upon the witching radiance of his love,
Upon her tulip cheeks, her musky locks,
Breathing the sweetness of a summer garden;
Upon the sparkling brightness of her rings,
Necklace, and bracelets, glittering on her arms.
His mien too was majestic--on his head

He wore a ruby crown, and near his breast
Was seen a belted dagger. Fondly she
With side-long glances marked his noble aspect,
The fine proportions of his graceful limbs,
His strength and beauty. Her enamoured heart
Suffused her cheek with blushes, every glance
Increased the ardent transports of her soul...

Rapunzel let down her tresses and the Witch climbed up.
Happy Hour Stories - Stories from Grimm's Fairy Tales, 1812.
Illustrated by J. Monsell

PETROSINELLA

(An Italian Tale)

Petrosinella (translating as 'Little Parsley') was written by Giambattista Basile (1566-1632), a Neapolitan poet and courtier. It was first published in his collection of Neapolitan fairy tales titled *Lo Cunto de li Cunti Overo lo Ttrattenemiento de Peccerille* (translating as 'The Tale of Tales, or Entertainment for Little Ones'), posthumously published in two volumes in 1634 and 1636.

Although neglected for some time, the work received a great deal of attention after the Brothers Grimm praised it highly as the first *national* collection of fairy tales. Many of the fairy tales that Basile collected are the oldest known variants in existence, including this – the first full-length printed version of the 'Rapunzel-Type' narrative. *Petrosinella* contains many elements subsequently replicated by the Brothers Grimm and other folklorists. Most notably is the uneven bargain of the mother forced to relinquish her daughter; the beautiful maiden with long hair (with obvious parallels to Rúdábeh), and the handsome Prince. Similarly to the Legend of Saint Barbara, Petrosinella escapes the witches tower (analogously to the confines of pagan religion), and the ogress (like the father) eventually meets a suitable punishment.

>————→

So great is my desire to keep the Princess amused, that the whole of the past night, when all were sound asleep and nobody stirred hand or foot, I have done nothing but turn over the old papers of my brain, and ransack ail the closets of my memory, choosing from among the stories which that good soul Mistress Chiarella Usciolo, my uncle's grandmother (whom Heaven take to glory!) used to tell, such as seemed most fitting to relate to you; and unless I have put on my spectacles upside down, I fancy they will give you pleasure; or, should they not serve, as armed squadrons, to drive away tedium from your mind, they will at least be as trumpets to incite my companions here to go forth to the field, with greater power than my poor strength possesses, to supply by the abundance of their wit the deficiencies of my discourse.

There was once upon a time a woman named Pascadozzia, who was in the family way; and as she was standing one day at a window, which looked into the garden of an ogress, she saw a beautiful bed of parsley, for which she took such a longing that she was on the point of fainting away; and being unable to resist her desire, she watched until the ogress went out, and then plucked a handful of it. But when the ogress came home, and was going to cook her pottage, she found that some one had been at the parsley, and said, "Ill luck to me but I'll catch this long-fingered rogue, and make him repent it, and teach him to his cost that every one should eat off his own platter, and not meddle with other folks' cups."

The poor woman went again and again down into the garden, until one morning the ogress met her, and in a furious rage exclaimed, "Have I caught you at last, you thief, you rogue! prithee do you pay the rent of the garden, that you come in this impudent way and steal my plants? by my faith, but I'll make you do penance without sending you to Rome!"

Poor Pascadozzia, in a terrible fright, began to make excuses, saying that neither from gluttony nor the craving of hunger had she been tempted by the devil to commit this fault, but from her being pregnant, and the fear she had lest the child should be born with a crop of parsley on its face; and she added that the ogress ought rather to thank her, for not having given her sore eyes.

"Words are but wind," answered the ogress; "I am not to be caught with such prattle; you have closed the balance-sheet of life, unless you promise to give me the child you bring forth, girl or boy, whichever it may be."

The Witch climbed up.
Hansel and Grethel and Other Tales, 1920
Illustrated by Arthur Rackham

For years she pined in vain.

Told Again - Old Tales Told Again, 1927.

Illustrated by A. H. Watson

Poor Pascadozzia, in order to escape the peril in which she found herself, swore with one hand upon another to keep the promise: so the ogress let her go free. But when her time was come, Pascadozzia gave birth to a little girl, so beautiful that she was a joy to look upon, who, from having a fine sprig of parsley on her bosom, was named Petrosinella. And the little girl grew from day to day, until when she was seven years old her mother sent her to school; and every time she went along the street and met the ogress, the old woman said to her, "Tell your mother to remember her promise." And she went on repeating this message so often, that the poor mother, having no longer patience to listen to the music, said one day to Petrosinella, "If you meet the old woman as usual, and she reminds you of the hateful promise, answer her, 'Take it!'"

When Petrosinella, who dreamt of no ill, met the ogress again, and heard her repeat the same words, she answered innocently as her mother had told her; where upon the ogress, seizing her by her hair, carried her off to a wood, which the horses of the Sun never entered, not having paid the toll to the pastures of those Shades. Then she put the poor girl into a tower, which she caused to arise by her art, and which had neither gate nor ladder, but only a little window, through which she ascended and descended by means of Petrosinella's hair, which was very long, as the sailor is used to run up and down the mast of a ship.

Now it happened one day, when the ogress had left the tower, that Petrosinella put her head out of the little window, and let loose her tresses in the sun; and the son of a prince passing by saw those two golden banners, which invited all souls to enlist under the standard of Love; and beholding with amazement in the midst of those gleaming waves a siren's face, that enchanted all hearts, he fell desperately in love with such wonderful beauty; and sending her a memorial of sighs, she de creed to receive him into favour. Matters went on so well with the prince, that there was soon a nodding of heads and a kissing of hands, a winking of eyes and bowing, thanks and offerings, hopes and promises, soft words and compliments. And when this had continued for several days, Petrosinella and the prince became so intimate that they made an appointment to meet, and agreed that it should be at night, when the Moon plays at hide with the Stars; and that Petrosinella should give the ogress some poppy-juice, and draw up the prince with her tresses. So when the appointed hour came, the prince went to the tower, where Petrosinella, letting fall her hair at a given signal, he seized it with both his hands, and cried, " Draw up!" And when he was drawn up, he crept through the little window into the chamber.

The next morning, before the Sun taught his steeds to leap through the hoop of the Zodiac, the prince descended by the same golden ladder, to go his way home. And having repeated these visits many times, a gossip of the ogress, who was for ever prying into things that did not concern her, and poking her nose into every corner, got to find out the secret, and told the ogress to be upon the look-out, for that Petrosinella made love with a certain youth, and she suspected that matters would go further; adding, that she saw what was going on, and feared they would be off and away before May. The ogress thanked her gossip for the information, and said she would take good care to stop up the road; and as to Petrosinella, it was moreover impossible for her to escape, as she had laid a spell upon her, so that, unless she had in her hand the three gallnuts which were in a rafter in the kitchen, it would be labour lost to at tempt to get away.

Whilst they were talking thus together, Petrosinella, who stood with her ears wide open, and had some suspicion of the gossip, overheard all that passed. And when Night had spread out her black garments to keep them from the moth, and the prince had come as usual, she made him climb on to the rafters and find the gallnuts, knowing well what effect they would have, as she had been enchanted by the ogress.

Then, having made a rope-ladder, they both descended to the ground, took to their heels, and scampered off towards the city. But the gossip happening to see them come out, set up a loud halloo, and began to shout and make such a noise

Then Rapunzel let down her tresses, and the Witch mounted up.
The Fairy Tales of Grimm, 1936.

Illustrated by Anne Anderson

"Ah!" said the Prince, "if that is the ladder one has to climb, I will try my luck."
Grimm's Fairy Tales, 1900.

Illustrated by Ernest Nister

that the ogress awoke; and seeing that Petrosinella had fled, she descended by the same ladder, which was fastened to the window, and set off running after the lovers, who, when they saw her coming at their heels faster than a horse let loose, gave themselves up for lost. But Petrosinella, recollecting the gallnuts, quickly threw one on the ground, and lo! instantly a Corsican bulldog started up,-O mother, such a terrible beast!-which with open jaws and barking loud flew at the ogress as if to swallow her at a mouthful. But the old woman, who was more cunning and spiteful than the devil, put her hand into her pocket, and pulling out a piece of bread, gave it to the dog, which made him hang his tail and allay his fury. Then she turned to run after the fugitives again; but Petrosinella, seeing her approach, threw the second gallnut on the ground, and lo! a fierce lion arose, who, lashing the earth with his tail, and shaking his mane, and opening wide his jaws a yard apart, was just preparing to make a slaughter of the ogress; when, turning quickly back, she stripped the skin off an ass that was grazing in the middle of a meadow, and ran at the lion, who, fancying it a real jackass, was so frightened that he bounded away as fast as he could.

The ogress, having leaped over this second ditch, turned again to pursue the poor lovers, who, hearing the clatter of her heels and seeing the cloud of dust that rose up to the sky, conjectured that she was coming again. But the old woman, who was every moment in dread lest the lion should pursue her, had not taken off the ass's skin; and when Petrosinella now threw down the third gallnut, there sprang up a wolf, who, without giving the ogress time to play any new trick, gobbled her up just as she was, in the shape of a jackass. So the lovers, being now freed from danger, went their way leisurely and quietly to the kingdom of the prince, where, with his father's free consent, he took Petrosinella to wife; and thus, after all these storms of fate, they experienced the truth, that

> "One hour in port, the sailor freed from fears
> Forgets the tempests of a hundred years."

RAPUNZEL

(A German Tale)

Rapunzel is a tale collected by the Brothers Grimm, (or *Die Brüder Grimm*), Jacob (1785 - 1863) and Wilhelm Grimm (1786 - 1859). It was first published in *Kinder und Hausmärchen* ('Children's and Household Tales') in 1812. *Kinder und Hausmärchen* was a pioneering collection of German folklore, and the Grimms built their anthology on the conviction that a national identity could be found in popular culture and with the common folk (*Volk*). Their first volumes were highly criticised however, because although they were called 'Children's Tales', they were not regarded as suitable for children, for both their scholarly information and frequently violent subject matter.

Akin to Basile's *Petrosinella* (meaning 'little parsely'), *Rapunzel* translates as a type of lettuce – the fated food that the mother craves. The Grimm's version differs from Basile's, in that the Prince, on climbing into the tower for the final time, finds not Rapunzel, but the evil sorceress. On making this discovery, he throws himself from the tower in despair, blinding himself on the thorns below. Like Rúdábeh and Saint Barbara, Rapunzel is kept in the tower not as punishment to the girl herself, but in order to guard the 'most beautiful child under the sun' by removing her from the outside world.

$$\longrightarrow$$

Once upon a time there was a man and a woman who had long, but to no avail, wished for a child. Finally the woman came to believe that the good Lord would fulfill her wish. Through the small rear window of these people's house they could see into a splendid garden that was filled with the most beautiful flowers and herbs. The garden was surrounded by a high wall, and no one dared enter, because it belonged to a sorceress who possessed great power and was feared by everyone.

One day the woman was standing at this window, and she saw a bed planted with the most beautiful rapunzel. It looked so fresh and green that she longed for some. It was her greatest desire to eat some of the rapunzel. This desire increased with every day, and not knowing how to get any, she became miserably ill.

Her husband was frightened, and asked her, "What ails you, dear wife?"

"Oh," she answered, "if I do not get some rapunzel from the garden behind our house, I shall die."

The man, who loved her dearly, thought, "Before you let your wife die, you must get her some of the rapunzel, whatever the cost."

So just as it was getting dark he climbed over the high wall into the sorceress's garden, hastily dug up a handful of rapunzel, and took it to his wife. She immediately made a salad from it, which she devoured eagerly. It tasted so very good to her that by the next day her desire for more had grown threefold. If she were to have any peace, the man would have to climb into the garden once again. Thus he set forth once again just as it was getting dark. But no sooner than he had climbed over the wall than, to his horror, he saw the sorceress standing there before him.

"How can you dare," she asked with an angry look, "to climb into my garden and like a thief to steal my rapunzel? You will pay for this."

I come Rapunzel!
Told Again - Old Tales Told Again, 1927.
Illustrated by A. H. Watson

Rapunzel.
Grimm's Fairy Stories, 1914.
Illustrated by Johnny Gruelle

"Oh," he answered, "Let mercy overrule justice. I came to do this out of necessity. My wife saw your rapunzel from our window, and such a longing came over her, that she would die, if she did not get some to eat."

The sorceress's anger abated somewhat, and she said, "If things are as you say, I will allow you to take as much rapunzel as you want. But under one condition: You must give me the child that your wife will bring to the world. It will do well, and I will take care of it like a mother."

In his fear the man agreed to everything.

When the woman gave birth, the sorceress appeared, named the little girl Rapunzel, and took her away. Rapunzel became the most beautiful child under the sun. When she was twelve years old, the fairy locked her in a tower that stood in a forest and that had neither a door nor a stairway, but only a tiny little window at the very top.

When the sorceress wanted to enter, she stood below and called out:

Rapunzel, Rapunzel,

Let down your hair to me.

Rapunzel had splendid long hair, as fine as spun gold. When she heard the sorceress's voice, she untied her braids, wound them around a window hook, let her hair fall twenty yards to the ground, and the sorceress climbed up it.

A few years later it happened that a king's son was riding through the forest. As he approached the tower he heard a song so beautiful that he stopped to listen. It was Rapunzel, who was passing the time by singing with her sweet voice. The prince wanted to climb up to her, and looked for a door in the tower, but none was to be found.

He rode home, but the song had so touched his heart that he returned to the forest every day and listened to it. One time, as he was thus standing behind a tree, he saw the sorceress approach, and heard her say:

Rapunzel, Rapunzel,

Let down your hair!

Then Rapunzel let down her strands of hair, and the sorceress climbed up them to her.

"If that is the ladder into the tower, then sometime I will try my luck."

And the next day, just as it was beginning to get dark, he went to the tower and called out:

Rapunzel, Rapunzel,

Let down your hair!

The hair fell down, and the prince climbed up.

At first Rapunzel was terribly frightened when a man such as she had never seen before came in to her. However, the prince began talking to her in a very friendly manner, telling her that his heart had been so touched by her singing that he could have no peace until he had seen her in person. Then Rapunzel lost her fear, and when he asked her if she would take him as her husband, she thought, "He would rather have me than would old Frau Gothel." She said yes and placed her hand into his.

Rapunzel.
Early Poems by William Morris, 1914.
Illustrated by Florence Harrison

Rapunzel.
Painting by Heinrich Lefler, 1905.

She said, "I would go with you gladly, but I do not know how to get down. Every time that you come, bring a strand of silk, from which I will weave a ladder. When it is finished I will climb down, and you can take me away on your horse." They arranged that he would come to her every evening, for the old woman came by day.

The sorceress did not notice what was happening until one day Rapunzel said to her, "Frau Gothel, tell me why it is that you are more difficult to pull up than is the young prince, who will be arriving any moment now?"

"You godless child," cried the sorceress. "What am I hearing from you? I thought I had removed you from the whole world, but you have deceived me nonetheless."

In her anger she grabbed Rapunzel's beautiful hair, wrapped it a few times around her left hand, grasped a pair of scissors with her right hand, and snip snap, cut it off. And she was so unmerciful that she took Rapunzel into a wilderness where she suffered greatly.

On the evening of the same day that she sent Rapunzel away, the fairy tied the cut-off hair to the hook at the top of the tower, and when the prince called out:

Rapunzel, Rapunzel,

Let down your hair!

She let down the hair.

The prince climbed up, but above, instead of his beloved Rapunzel, he found the sorceress, who peered at him with poisonous and evil looks.

"Aha!" she cried scornfully. "You have come for your Mistress Darling, but that beautiful bird is no longer sitting in her nest, nor is she singing any more. The cat got her, and will scratch your eyes out as well. You have lost Rapunzel. You will never see her again."

The prince was overcome with grief, and in his despair he threw himself from the tower. He escaped with his life, but the thorns into which he fell poked out his eyes. Blind, he wandered about in the forest, eating nothing but grass and roots, and doing nothing but weeping and wailing over the loss of his beloved wife. Thus he wandered about miserably for some years, finally happening into the wilderness where Rapunzel lived miserably with the twins that she had given birth to.

He heard a voice and thought it was familiar. He advanced toward it, and as he approached, Rapunzel recognized him, and crying, threw her arms around his neck. Two of her tears fell into his eyes, and they became clear once again, and he could see as well as before. He led her into his kingdom, where he was received with joy, and for a long time they lived happily and satisfied.

And she let down her hair, and the King's Son climbed up by it.
Grimm's Fairy Tales - Stories and Tales of Elves, Goblins and Fairies, 1917.
Illustrated by Louis Rhead

The Maid and the Negress

(A Portuguese Tale)

This story comes from an anthology of *Portuguese Folk Tales*, compiled by Zófimo Consiglieri Pedroso (1851 - 1910), a Portuguese historian, writer, ethnographer and folklorist. He was devoted to the study of ethnography (the systematic study of people and cultures) and introduced anthropology as an academic pursuit to Portugal, studying the country's myths, popular traditions and superstitions. Ironically, for a book dedicated to Portuguese culture and story-telling, the book was actually issued in England (in 1878) *before* its native publication.

This particular tale reflects the extreme racism which was prevalent in nineteenth century Portugal. This was largely the result of ancient racial tensions, as the Muslim Moors, Jews and the Christian Mozarabs, had been expelled from the continent during the 'Reconquista' and the expansion of the newly founded Kingdom of Portugal in the twelfth and thirteenth centuries. In this variant on the 'Rapunzel' narrative, the maiden is imprisoned in a tower, but it is the witch (not the prince) who happens to pass-by. The main villain though is the 'negress', who impersonates the fair maiden and consequently marries the prince.

>————→

There was once a maiden who was imprisoned in a tower. She was very much attached to a prince, who used to come every afternoon to speak to her. This girl would let down her hair from the tower, and by this means the prince was enabled to come up and hold a conversation with her. One day, just as

O Rapunzel, Rapunzel! Let down thine hair!
Grimm's Fairy Tales, 1882.
Illustrated by Walter Crane

a witch happened to be passing that way, she saw the prince ascend. What should she do? She came next day to the place, earlier than the prince was in the habit of doing, and, imitating the prince's voice and speech, she called out to the girl. The girl threw down her hair as usual, and the witch caught hold of the long tress and ascended. She then commenced to tell the maiden not to care for the prince, and to discard him, and in fact gave her much bad advice; and when she found that it was near the hour when the prince would arrive as usual at the tower, she again laid hold of the girl's hair and slipped down to the ground.

As soon as the maiden saw the prince she recounted to him all the witch had said to her, and how she had deceived her in order to ascend the tower. When the prince heard this he at once ordered a carriage in order to run away with the maiden. Before the girl left the tower she took leave of everything in it, but she forgot to take leave of the besom and the broomstick. She took away with her a glass with water, a little bag with stones, and another with sand, and she ran away. A little while after the witch came again to the foot of the tower, and began calling out to the girl as she had done the day before. To this the table and the chairs replied, "The maiden is very ill." But the broomstick and the besom which had remained, very much hurt and angry on account of the girl not having taken leave of them, came to the window and said to the witch, "What they say is not true; the girl ran away with the prince!"

As soon as the witch knew this, she began to run to overtake her. The girl, who felt distrustful of the consequences, put her head out of the carriage to look out, and when she saw the witch following she emptied the bag of sand she had with her, and immediately a sand waste was formed. The witch found great difficulty in getting over the sand, but she managed to pass it, and still continued to run after the carriage. When the maiden saw that the witch was nearly overtaking her, she threw out the stones she carried in the other bag, and instantly a great wall rose up. The witch found great difficulty in getting over this wall, but succeeded in clearing it, and continued running to reach the carriage. But when the maiden saw that the witch had succeeded in getting over the wall, and was nearly upon her, she threw out the water she carried in the glass, and instantly a large wide river was formed; this time, however, the witch was unable to pass.

When the prince arrived at the gates of the city, he said to the maiden, "You must remain here on the top of this tree whilst I go and summon my court together, for I cannot make my public entry without them;" and he gave her his word that he would return for her. The maiden remained on the top of the tree, which grew close to a fountain, and whose branches fell over it. A little while after a negro woman came with a pitcher for water: she saw the reflection of the girl's face upon it, and, thinking it was her own figure, she saw, she cried out, "Oh! beautiful negress! break the pitcher!" She knocked the pitcher against the fountain and broke it. She then went away, but came back with another pitcher. She looked upon the limpid water, and seeing the girl's reflection upon it, she repeated, "Oh! beautiful negress! break the pitcher!" and again she broke the pitcher. The negro woman departed, and a third time returned with a tin jug. She looked towards the fountain, and again seeing the reflection of the maiden's figure, she said, "Oh! beautiful negress! break the pitcher!" But, as the pitcher was made of tin, she could not succeed in breaking it as she knocked it against the fountain.

The negro woman, already very angry because she could not break the jug, said to herself, "Oh, what manner of a beautiful negro woman must this be that cannot break the pitcher!" She looked up to the tree, and, on seeing the maiden, she said, "Oh, poor girl! you are up there quite by yourself; would you like me to stay with you?" And she also went up the tree. She inquired of the maiden what she was doing there, and then said to her, "Oh, my girl! what a beautiful head of hair you have got! Would you like me to comb you?" Saying this, she pierced her head with a long pin. The girl at once became transformed

Rapunzel.
Painting by Isobel Lilian Gloag, Date Unknown.

into a dove, and flew about. When the prince returned he was much surprised at this, and said, "What ails you, my girl, who were so beautiful, and now you are so black?" "What would you have?" replied the black woman; "you left me here exposed to the heat of the sun, and I became sunburnt." The prince had certainly doubts about the truth of this, as was convinced that this negress was not the girl he had left there; yet, as he had given his word to the maid, he took her to the palace and married her.

Every day a beautiful dove came to the garden which would coo, "Oh, gardener, how does the prince fare with his black Maria?" and the gardener replied, "Pretty well; be off." When the gardener met the prince coming into the garden, he related what had taken place. The prince told him that when the dove should come on the following day he was to lay a snare of ribbon to catch her. The next day the dove returned. "Oh, gardener, how does the prince fare with black Maria?" she cried. The gardener then threw at her the lasso of ribbon, but the dove merely replied, "Ha! ha! ha! Snares of ribbon were not made to catch me!" and flew away. When the prince came to inquire what had occurred, the gardener told him what the dove had said. The prince then said, "To-morrow throw over her a snare made of silver." The dove returned again and said, "Ha! ha! ha! Snares of silver are not made for me!" and flew away. And when the prince heard this, he ordered the gardener to lay a golden snare; and the little dove this time was caught. The gardener then took her to the prince. But when the black woman saw the dove she began telling the prince to kill it; the prince however would not, because he had already grown very fond of the little dove, and esteemed her more and more.

One day as the prince was petting her he discovered a pin stuck in her pretty head which he at once extricated, and instantly the dove was transformed into the maiden. She then related to the prince all that had taken place, and he told her he would marry her. After this the prince asked her what she wished him to do to the black woman. The maiden replied that he should kill her and with her bones make bed-steps for her to climb into her bed, and with her skin to make a drum.

Rapunzel.

The Defence of Guenevere and Other Poems by William Morris, 1904.

Illustrated by Illustrated by Jessie M. King

PRUNELLA

(A British Tale)

The story of *Prunella* was written down by the Scottish folklorist Andrew Lang (1844 - 1912), in *The Grey Fairy Book* (1900). Lang produced twelve collections of fairy tales in total, each volume distinguished by its own colour. Although he did not collect the stories himself from oraltellings, Lang is only rivalled by Madame d'Aulnoy (1650 - 1705) for the sheer variety of sources and cultural diversity included in his anthologies.

Lang did not provide any information on Prunella's provenance, though it can be assumed it derives chiefly from the Italian *Petrosinella*. Lang was concerned that the graphic nature of the violence was unfit for younger readers, and so changed details such as the ogress's grizzly ending (being eaten by a wolf), with the witch 'merely' falling down the stairs. Like Basile's tale, the child is seven years old when she is taken by the witch, her 'innocent' nature being highlighted in the narrative. Prunella (akin to Petrosinella/Parsley and Rapunzel/Lettuce), is actually a type of herbaceous plant, traditionally used in herbal medicine, as well as bearing obvious resemblance to a 'prune' (the plums that Prunella eats). Instead of being locked in a tower, in this tale the witch sets the young girl a series of seemingly impossible tasks...

———➤

There was once upon a time a woman who had an only daughter. When the child was about seven years old she used to pass every day, on her way to school, an orchard where there was a wild plum tree, with delicious ripe plums hanging from the branches. Each morning the child would pick one, and put it into her pocket to eat at school. For this reason she was called Prunella. Now, the orchard belonged to a witch. One day the witch noticed the child gathering a plum, as she passed along the road. Prunella did it quite innocently, not knowing that she was doing wrong in taking the fruit that hung close to the roadside. But the witch was furious, and next day hid herself behind the hedge, and when Prunella came past, and put out her hand to pluck the fruit, she jumped out and seized her by the arm.

'Ah! You little thief!' she exclaimed. 'I have caught you at last. Now you will have to pay for your misdeeds.'

The poor child, half dead with fright, implored the old woman to forgive her, assuring her that she did not know she had done wrong, and promising never to do it again. But the witch had no pity, and she dragged Prunella into her house, where she kept her till the time should come when she could have her revenge.

As the years passed Prunella grew up into a very beautiful girl. Now her beauty and goodness, instead of softening the witch's heart, aroused her hatred and jealousy.

One day she called Prunella to her, and said: 'Take this basket, go to the well, and bring it back to me filled with water. If you don't I will kill you.'

The girl took the basket, went and let it down into the well again and again. But her work was lost labour. Each time, as she drew up the basket, the water streamed out of it. At last, in despair, she gave it up, and leaning against the well she began to cry bitterly, when suddenly she heard a voice at her side saying 'Prunella, why are you crying?'

Zal meets Rudaba.
Old Persian Manuscript of the Shahnama, *c.* 8th century AH.
Illustrator Unknown

The Prince at once climbed up.
Grimm's Fairy Tales - Retold in One-Syllable Words, 1899.
Illustrated by R. André

Turning round she beheld a handsome youth, who looked kindly at her, as if he were sorry for her trouble.

'Who are you,' she asked, 'and how do you know my name ?'

'I am the son of the witch,' he replied, 'and my name is Bensiabel. I know that she is determined that you shall die, but I promise you that she shall not carry out her wicked plan. Will you give me a kiss, if I fill your basket?'

'No,' said Prunella, 'I will not give you a kiss, because you are the son of a witch.'

'Very well,' replied the youth sadly. 'Give me your basket and I will fill it for you.' And he dipped it into the well, and the water stayed in it. Then the girl returned to the house, carrying the basket filled with water. When the witch saw it, she became white with rage, and exclaimed 'Bensiabel must have helped you.' And Prunella looked down, and said nothing.

'Well, we shall see who will win in the end,' said the witch, in a great rage.

The following day she called the girl to her and said:

'Take this sack of wheat. I am going out for a little; by the time I return I shall expect you to have made it into bread. If you have not done it I will kill you.' Having said this she left the room, closing and locking the door behind her.

Poor Prunella did not know what to do. It was impossible for her to grind the wheat, prepare the dough, and bake the bread, all in the short time that the witch would be away. At first she set to work bravely, but when she saw how hopeless her task was, she threw herself on a chair, and began to weep bitterly.

She was roused from her despair by hearing Bensiabel's voice at her side saying: 'Prunella, Prunella, do not weep like that. If you will give me a kiss I will make the bread, and you will be saved.'

'I will not kiss the son of a witch,' replied Prunella.

But Bensiabel took the wheat from her, and ground it, and made the dough, and when the witch returned the bread was ready baked in the oven.

Turning to the girl, with fury in her voice, she said 'Bensiabel must have been here and helped you;' and Prunella looked down, and said nothing.

'We shall see who will win in the end,' said the witch, and her eyes blazed with anger.

Next day she called the girl to her and said: 'Go to my sister, who lives across the mountains. She will give you a casket, which you must bring back to me.' This she said knowing that her sister, who was a still more cruel and wicked witch than herself, would never allow the girl to return, but would imprison her and starve her to death. But Prunella did not suspect anything, and set out quite cheerfully. On the way she met Bensiabel.

'Where are you going, Prunella?' he asked.

'I am going to the sister of my mistress, from whom I am to fetch a casket.'

'Oh poor, poor girl!' said Bensiabel. 'You are being sent straight to your death. Give me a kiss, and I will save you.'

But again Prunella answered as before, 'I will not kiss the son of a witch.'

Rapunzel, Rapunzel, let down your golden hair.
The Red Fairy Book, 1890.
Illustrated by H. J. Ford

The King's son climbed up.

Grimm's Fairy Tales, 1922.

Illustrated by R. Emmett Owen

'Nevertheless, I will save your life,' said Bensiabel, for I love you better than myself. Take this flagon of oil, this loaf of bread, this piece of rope, and this broom. When you reach the witch's house, oil the hinges of the door with the contents of the flagon, and throw the loaf of bread to the great fierce mastiff, who will come to meet you. When you have passed the dog, you will see in the courtyard a miserable woman trying in vain to let down a bucket into the well with her plaited hair. You must give her the rope. In the kitchen you will find a still more miserable woman trying to clean the hearth with her tongue; to her you must give the broom. You will see the casket on the top of a cupboard, take it as quickly as you can, and leave the house without a moment's delay. If you do all this exactly as I have told you, you will not be killed.'

So Prunella, having listened carefully to his instructions, did just what he had told her. She reached the house, oiled the hinges of the door, threw the loaf to the dog, gave the poor woman at the well the rope, and the woman in the kitchen the broom, caught up the casket from the top of the cupboard, and fled with it out of the house. But the witch heard her as she ran away, and rushing to the window called out to the woman in the kitchen: 'Kill that thief, I tell you!'

But the woman replied: 'I will not kill her, for she has given me a broom, whereas you forced me to clean the hearth with my tongue.'

Then the witch called out in fury to the woman at the well: 'Take the girl, I tell you, and fling her into the water, and drown her!'

But the woman answered: 'No, I will not drown her, for she gave me this rope, whereas you forced me to use my hair to let down the bucket to draw water.'

Then the witch shouted to the dog to seize the girl and hold her fast; but the dog answered: 'No, I will not seize her, for she gave me a loaf of bread, whereas you let me starve with hunger.'

The witch was so angry that she nearly choked, as she called out: 'Door, bang upon her, and keep her a prisoner.'

But the door answered: 'I won't, for she has oiled my hinges, so that they move quite easily, whereas you left them all rough and rusty.'

And so Prunella escaped, and, with the casket under her arm, reached the house of her mistress, who, as you may believe, was as angry as she was surprised to see the girl standing before her, looking more beautiful than ever. Her eyes flashed, as in furious tones she asked her, 'Did you meet Bensiabel?'

But Prunella looked down, and said nothing.

'We shall see,' said the witch, 'who will win in the end. Listen, there are three cocks in the hen-house; one is yellow, one black, and the third is white. If one of them crows during the night you must tell me which one it is. Woe to you if you make a mistake. I will gobble you up in one mouthful.'

Now Bensiabel was in the room next to the one where Prunella slept. At midnight she awoke hearing a cock crow.

'Which one was that?' shouted the witch.

Then, trembling, Prunella knocked on the wall and whispered: 'Bensiabel, Bensiabel, tell me, which cock crowed?'

'Will you give me a kiss if I tell you?' he whispered back through the wall.

Rapunzel.

Grimm's Fairy Tales - Stories and Tales of Elves, Goblins and Fairies, 1917.

Illustrated by Louis Rhead

But she answered 'No.'

Then he whispered back to her: 'Nevertheless, I will tell you. It was the yellow cock that crowed.'

The witch, who had noticed the delay in Prunella's answer, approached her door calling angrily: 'Answer at once, or I will kill you.'

So Prunella answered: 'It was the yellow cock that crowed.'

And the witch stamped her foot and gnashed her teeth.

Soon after another cock crowed. 'Tell me now which one it is,' called the witch. And, prompted by Bensiabel, Prunella answered: 'That is the black cock.'

A few minutes after the crowing was heard again, and the voice of the witch demanding 'Which one was that?'

And again Prunella implored Bensiabel to help her. But this time he hesitated, for he hoped that Prunella might forget that he was a witch's son, and promise to give him a kiss. And as he hesitated he heard an agonised cry from the girl: 'Bensiabel, Bensiabel, save me! The witch is coming, she is close to me, I hear the gnashing of her teeth!'

With a bound Bensiabel opened his door and flung himself against the witch. He pulled her back with such force that she stumbled, and falling headlong, dropped down dead at the foot of the stairs.

Then, at last, Prunella was touched by Bensiabel's goodness and kindness to her, and she became his wife, and they lived happily ever after.

Snip, snap, she cut off all her beautiful tresses.
Hansel and Gretel and Other Stories, 1925.
Illustrated by Kay Nielsen

Juan and Clotilde

(A Philippine Tale)

Juan and Clotilde was written down by Professor Dean Spruill Fansler (1885 - 1945). It was published in *Filipino Popular Tales* in 1921, a book which met with considerable critical acclaim. Fansler collected the stories whilst involved in educational work in the Philippines, and attempted to replicate the tales 'exactly as they are told by the Filipinos' (excepting their translation into English).

Many of the stories were of ancient origin, though several also showed the influence of European Christianity, largely bought to the Philippines with the arrival of the Spanish (present from the arrival of Ferdinand Magellan in 1521, until the Spanish-American War which ended Spanish rule in 1898). The story of *Juan and Clotilde* is one such example, with the beautiful young Clotilde being locked in a high and inaccessible tower by the magician. The 'prince' character does not climb up the fair maiden's hair however, but creates a ladder made of ropes and nails, before escaping on an enchanted winged horse.

———➤

In ages vastly remote there lived in a distant land a king of such prowess and renown, that his name was known throughout the four regions of the compass. His name was Ludovico. His power was increased twofold by his attachment to an aged magician, to whom he was tied by strong bonds of friendship...

She made the tresses fast above to the window latch.

Fairy Tales from Grimm, 1894.

Illustrated by Gordon Browne

Ludovico had an extremely lovely daughter by the name of Clotilde. Ever since his arrival at the palace the magician had been passionately in love with her; but his extreme old age and his somewhat haughty bearing were obstacles in his path to success. Whenever he made love to her, she turned aside, and listened instead to the thrilling tales told by some wandering minstrel.

The magician finally succumbed to the infirmities of old age, his life made more burdensome by his repeated disappointments. He left to the king three enchanted winged horses; to the princess, two magic necklaces of exactly the same appearance, of inimitable workmanship and of priceless worth. Nor did the magician fail to wreak vengeance on the cause of his death. Before he expired, he locked Clotilde and the three magic horses in a high tower inaccessible to any human being. She was to remain in this enchanted prison until some man succeeded in setting her free.

Naturally, King Ludovico wanted to see his daughter before the hour of his death, which was fast approaching. He offered large sums of money, together with his crown and Clotilde's hand, to anybody who could set her free. Hundreds of princes tried, but in vain. The stone walls of the tower were of such a height, that very few birds, even, could fly over them. But a deliverer now rose from obscurity and came into prominence. This man was an uneducated but persevering peasant named Juan. He possessed a graceful form, herculean frame, good heart, and unrivalled ingenuity. His two learned older brothers tried to scale the walls of the tower, but fared no better than the others.

At last Juan's turn came. His parents and his older brothers expostulated with him not to go, for what could a man unskilled in the fine arts do? But Juan, in the hope of setting the princess free, paid no attention to their advice. He took as many of the biggest nails as he could find, a very long rope, and a strong hammer. As he lived in a town several miles distant from the capital, he had to make the trip on horseback.

One day Juan set out with all his equipment. On the way he met his disappointed second brother returning after a vain attempt. The older brother tried in every way he could to divert Juan from his purpose. Now, Juan's parents, actuated partly by a sense of shame if he should fail, and partly by a deep-seated hatred, had poisoned his food without his knowledge. When he felt hungry, he suspected them of some evil intention: so before eating he gave his horse some of his provisions. The poor creature died on the road amidst terrible sufferings, and Juan was obliged to finish the journey on foot.

When he arrived at the foot of the tower, he drove a nail into the wall. Then he tied one end of his rope to this spike. In this way he succeeded in making a complete ladder of nails and rope to the top of the tower. He looked for Clotilde, who met him with her eyes flooded with tears. As a reward for his great services to her, she gave him one of the magic necklaces. While they were whispering words of love in each other's ears, they heard a deafening noise at the bottom of the tower.

"Rush for safety to your ladder!" cried Clotilde. "One of the fiendish friends of the magician is going to kill you."

But, alas! some wanton hand had pulled out the nails; and this person was none other then Juan's second brother. "I am a lost man," said Juan.

"Mount one of the winged horses in the chamber adjoining mine," said Clotilde.

So Juan got on one of the animals without knowing where to go. The horse flew from the tower with such velocity, that Juan had to close his eyes. His breath was almost taken away. In a few seconds, however, he was landed in a country entirely strange to his eyes.

To you Rapunzel is lost; you will never see her again.
The Fairy Tales of Grimm, 1936.
Illustrated by Anne Anderson

After long years of struggle with poverty and starvation, Juan was at last able to make his way back to his native country. He went to live in a town just outside the walls of the capital. A rich old man named Telesforo hired him to work on his farm. Juan's excellent service and irreproachable conduct won the good will of his master, who adopted him as his son.

At about this time King Ludovico gave out proclamations stating that any one who could exactly match his daughter's necklace should be his son-in-law. Thousands tried, but they tried in vain. Even the most dexterous and experienced smiths were baffled in their attempts to produce an exact counterfeit. When word of the royal proclamations was brought to Juan, he decided to try.

One day he pretended to be sick, and he asked Telesforo to go to the palace to get Clotilde's necklace. The old man, who was all ready to serve his adopted son, went that very afternoon and borrowed the necklace, so that he might try to copy it. When he returned with the magic article, Juan jumped from his bed and kissed his father. After supper Juan went to his room and locked himself in. Then he took from his pocket the necklace which Clotilde had given him in the tower, and compared it carefully with the borrowed one. When he saw that they did not differ in any respect, he took a piece of iron and hammered it until midnight.

Early the next morning Juan wrapped the two magic necklaces in a silk handkerchief, and told the old man to take them to the king.

"By the aid of the Lord!" exclaimed Clotilde when her father the king unwrapped the necklaces, "my lover is here again. This necklace," she said, touching the one she had given Juan, "is not a counterfeit: for it is written in the magician's book of black art that no human being shall be able to imitate either of the magic necklaces. -- Where is the owner of this necklace, old man?" she said, turning to Telesforo.

The Prince took his songbird and the little twins too, and together they rode away to his kingdom.

Tales from Grimm, 1936.

Illustrated by Wanda Gag

"He is at home," said Telesforo with a bow.

"Go and bring him to the palace," said Clotilde.

Within a quarter of an hour Juan arrived. After paying due respect to the king, Juan embraced Clotilde affectionately. They were married in the afternoon, and the festivities continued for nine days and nine nights. Juan was made crown prince, and on the death of King Ludovico he succeeded to the throne. King Juan and Queen Clotilde lived to extreme old age in peace and perfect happiness.

The Golden Age of Illustration

The 'Golden age of Illustration' refers to a period customarily defined as lasting from the latter quarter of the nineteenth century until just after the First World War. In this period of no more than fifty years the popularity, abundance and most importantly the unprecedented upsurge in quality of illustrated works marked an astounding change in the way that publishers, artists and the general public came to view this hitherto insufficiently esteemed art form.

Until the latter part of the nineteenth century, the work of illustrators was largely proffered anonymously, and in England it was only after Thomas Bewick's pioneering technical advances in wood engraving that it became common to acknowledge the artistic and technical expertise of book and magazine illustrators. Although widely regarded as the patriarch of the *Golden Age*, Walter Crane (1845-1915) started his career as an anonymous illustrator – gradually building his reputation through striking designs, famous for their sharp outlines and flat tints of colour. Like many other great illustrators to follow, Crane operated within many different mediums; a lifelong disciple of William Morris and a member of the Arts and Crafts Movement, he designed all manner of objects including wallpaper, furniture, ceramic ware and even whole interiors. This incredibly important and inclusive phase of British design proved to have a lasting impact on illustration both in the United Kingdom and Europe as well as America.

The artists involved in the Arts and Crafts Movement attempted to counter the ever intruding Industrial Revolution (the first wave of which lasted roughly from 1750-1850) by bringing the values of beautiful and inventive craftsmanship back into the sphere of everyday life. It must be noted that around the turn of the century the boundaries between what would today be termed 'fine art' as opposed to 'crafts' and 'design' were far more fluid and in many cases non-operational, and many illustrators had lucrative painterly careers in addition to their design work. The Romanticism of the *Pre Raphaelite Brotherhood* combined with the intricate curvatures of the *Art Nouveaux* movement provided influential strands running through most illustrators work. The latter especially so for the Scottish illustrator Anne Anderson (1874-1930) as well as the Dutch artist Kay Nielson (1886-1957), who was also inspired by the stunning work of Japanese artists such as Hiroshige.

One of the main accomplishments of nineteenth century illustration lay in its ability to reach far wider numbers than the traditional 'high arts'. In 1892 the American critic William A. Coffin praised the new medium for popularising art; 'more has been done through the medium of illustrated literature… to make the masses of people realise that there is such a thing as art and that it is worth caring about'. Commercially, illustrated publications reached their zenith with the burgeoning 'Gift Book' industry which emerged in the first decade of the twentieth century. The first widely distributed gift book was published in 1905. It comprised of Washington Irving's short story *Rip Van Winkle* with the addition of 51 colour plates by a true master of illustration; Arthur Rackham. Rackham created each plate by first painstakingly drawing his subject in a sinuous pencil line before applying an ink layer – then he used layer upon layer of delicate watercolours to build up the romantic yet calmly ethereal results on which his reputation was constructed. Although Rackham is now one of the most recognisable names in illustration, his delicate palette owed no small debt to Kate Greenaway (1846-1901) – one of the first female illustrators whose pioneering and incredibly subtle use of the watercolour medium resulted in her election to the Royal Institute of Painters in Water Colours, in 1889.

The year before Arthur Rackam's illustrations for *Rip Van Winkle* were published, a young and aspiring French artist by the name of Edmund Dulac

(1882-1953) came to London and was to create a similarly impressive legacy. His timing could not have been more fortuitous. Several factors converged around the turn of the century which allowed illustrators and publishers alike a far greater freedom of creativity than previously imagined. The origination of the 'colour separation' practice meant that colour images, extremely faithful to the original artwork could be produced on a grand scale. Dulac possessed a rigorously painterly background (more so than his contemporaries) and was hence able to utilise the new technology so as to allow the colour itself to refine and define an object as opposed to the traditional pen and ink line. It has been estimated that in 1876 there was only one 'colour separation' firm in London, but by 1900 this number had rocketed to fifty. This improvement in printing quality also meant a reduction in labour, and coupled with the introduction of new presses and low-cost supplies of paper this meant that publishers could for the first time afford to pay high wages for highly talented artists.

Whilst still in the U.K, no survey of the *Golden Age of Illustration* would be complete without a mention of the Heath-Robinson brothers. Charles Robinson was renowned for his beautifully detached style, whether in pen and ink or sumptuous watercolours. William (the youngest) was to later garner immense fame for his carefully constructed yet tortuous machines operated by comical, intensely serious attendants. After World War One, the Robinson brothers numbered among the few artists of the Golden Age who continued to regularly produce illustrated works. But as we move towards the United States, one illustrator - Howard Pyle (1853-1911) stood head and shoulders above his contemporaries as the most distinguished illustrator of the age. From 1880 onwards Pyle illustrated over 100 volumes, yet it was not quantity which ensured his precedence over other American (and European) illustrators, but quality.

Pyle's sumptuous illustrations benefitted from a meticulous composition process livened with rich colour and deep recesses, providing a visual framework in which tales such as *Robin Hood* and *The Four Volumes of the Arthurian Cycle* could come to life. These are publications which remain continuous good sellers up till the present day. His flair and originality combined with a thoroughness of planning and execution were principles which he passed onto his many pupils at the *Drexel Institute of Arts and Sciences*. Two such pupils were Jessie Willcox Smith (1863-1935) who went on to illustrate books such as *The Water Babies* and *At the Back of North Wind* and perhaps most famously Maxfield Parrish (1870-1966) who became famed for luxurious colour (most remarkably demonstrated in his blue paintings) and imaginative designs; practices in no short measure gleaned from his tutor. As an indication of Parrish's popularity, in 1925 it was estimated that one fifth of American households possessed a Parrish reproduction.

As is evident from this brief introduction to the 'Golden Age of Illustration', it was a period of massive technological change and artistic ingenuity. The legacy of this enormously important epoch lives on in the present day – in the continuing popularity and respect afforded to illustrators, graphic and fine artists alike. This *Origins of Fairy Tales from Around the World* series will hopefully provide a fascinating insight into an era of intense historical and creative development, bringing both little known stories, and the art that has accompanied them, back to life.

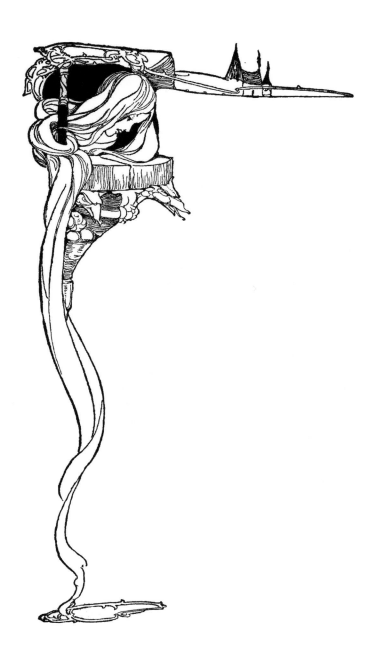

Printed in Great Britain
by Amazon